Lottie the Little Pony

As Emma saw the pony step out of the trailer, her mouth fell open in surprise. Her heart sank with disappointment too. *Is that really Lottie?* she wondered. She looks so *small*.

Titles in Jenny Dale's PONY TALES™ series

All of Jenny Dale's PONY TALES books can be ordered at your local bookshop or are available by post from Book Service by Post (tel: 01624 675137)

Lottie the Little Pony

by Jenny Dale

Illustrated by Frank Rodgers

A Working Partners Book

MACMILLAN CHILDREN'S BOOKS

Special thanks to Heather Maisner

First published 2000 by Macmillan Children's Books
a division of Macmillan Publishers Limited
25 Eccleston Place, London SW1W 9NF
Basingstoke and Oxford
www.macmillan.co.uk

Associated companies throughout the world

Created by Working Partners Limited
London W6 0QT

ISBN 0 330 37472 9

Copyright © Working Partners Limited 2000
Illustrations copyright © Frank Rodgers 2000

JENNY DALE'S PONY TALES is a trade mark
owned by Working Partners Ltd.

1 3 5 7 9 8 6 4 2

A CIP catalogue record for this book is available from
the British Library.

Typeset by SX Composing DTP, Rayleigh, Essex
Printed and bound in Great Britain by Mackays of Chatham plc, Kent

Chapter One

Emma Dodd lay asleep in her
bedroom, dreaming. She'd had the
same dream for almost two years:
her family had moved to a new
house with a big field next to it.
And in the field was a shed – a
shed big enough for a pony.

In her dream Emma heard a

gentle neigh and pounding hooves. She looked out of the window and saw . . .

Lottie!

Lottie was a Shetland pony, who lived with Emma's gran in Scotland. When Emma had gone to stay in Scotland two years ago, Granny Dodd had seen what good friends Emma and Lottie had become. She had said, "I'm getting a bit old to look after little Lottie now. If ever your mum and dad move to a home with space for Lottie, then she can come and live with you."

And now, as Emma woke, she felt a thrill of excitement. After all this time, the dream was about to come true! She rolled out of bed, went over to her bedroom window and pulled back the curtain a little.

Outside was a field – with a shed – and Lottie was coming to live there!

Emma and her family had moved to a new house last week – a house with much more space. Granny Dodd had been true to her

word. Lottie was on her way today!

Emma remembered every bit of that lovely long stay at Granny Dodd's two years before . . .

Each morning, as soon as she'd woken up, before she'd even had her breakfast, Emma had run out to meet Lottie.

As soon as Lottie had seen her, she'd cantered across and nuzzled against Emma with her soft grey nose.

When Emma had trotted round the field on Lottie's back, she'd never wanted to be anywhere else in the world.

Every evening, Emma would brush Lottie's thick, woolly coat and talk to her. "If only you could come and live with me," she'd said. "I'd be so happy."

But for two whole years after that, Emma and her mum and dad and little brother, Jim, had carried on living in the middle of town. Their house was nice, but the garden was too small – even for a little pony.

Then, a few weeks ago, everything had changed. Emma's mum had got a new job, and they were finally able to move to the other side of town – near the country. A new house had been found – with a field and a shed! All Emma needed now was Lottie!

Up in Scotland, Granny Dodd had been grooming Lottie. She said,

"I've got some exciting news for you, my lovely little lass."

"Oh, really?" Lottie whickered, nuzzling her owner's arm. "Is it something to do with apples?" Lottie loved apples. She pushed her soft nose into Granny Dodd's coat pocket. But the thing sticking out of her pocket didn't look or smell like an apple. It was flat and white and didn't smell of anything at all.

Granny Dodd smiled and took out a letter. "This is from Emma's mum and dad," she told Lottie. "It says that you can go and live with Emma now."

She stroked Lottie's shaggy mane and beamed. "You'd like that, wouldn't you, Lottie?

Someone to ride you and have fun with?"

Lottie whinnied with excitement. She loved kind old Granny Dodd, and would miss her. But what fun to live with Emma and be ridden by her every day!

The last time Lottie had seen Emma – ages and ages ago – Emma had given her a big hug and promised, "I'll nag Mum and Dad to move to a house with a field. Gran says that you can come and live with us then. Won't that be fantastic?"

Lottie had whinnied her agreement. But that had been so long ago. Granny Dodd had been down to London to visit Emma's family a few times since then, but Emma had never come back to stay at Granny Dodd's house. Sometimes Lottie had wondered if Emma even remembered her.

But now Lottie knew that Emma had!

Chapter Two

When Lottie's grooming was finished, she galloped across the field to Noah, the pony who shared her field. "I can't believe it – I'm going to live with Emma," she whinnied.

"Oh, lovely!" neighed Noah. "I remember her – she was fun! I'll miss you, but it'll be great for you to have someone to ride you every day."

"Yes!" whinnied Lottie. "Emma loved going for rides around the field. She never wanted to get off! But I didn't mind. She was so light, I could hardly feel her!"

A few days later, Granny Dodd drove the car and trailer into the field and called out to Lottie. It was time to leave.

Lottie snorted and cantered across. Then she stopped to look once more at the fields and trees that she'd known for as long as she could remember. She was sad to be leaving her old home.

Granny Dodd reached out and gave Lottie a hug. "I'm going to miss you, lass," she whispered. "I've had you since you were a tiny foal."

"And I'll miss you too," Lottie whickered against Granny Dodd's cheek.

"But I'll still see you sometimes

when I come and visit Emma and her family," Granny Dodd added, smiling.

Noah raced across the field to say goodbye. "Have a safe trip," he neighed. "It won't be the same here without you!"

Lottie whickered goodbye, then Granny Dodd led her into the trailer.

As the engine started up and the trailer moved forward, Lottie shook her head and snorted with excitement.

That same morning, many miles away, Emma decided there was no point in going back to bed. She would never fall asleep again. She pulled the bedroom curtains open.

Sunlight filled the room. So did her little brother Jim's voice, as he came running in. "I can't sleep!" he cried. "When is the pony going to get here?" Jim couldn't remember Lottie – he was only three when they'd had the long holiday in Scotland. But he was excited about having a pony come to live with them, just the same.

"Not for hours, yet," Emma told him. "Granny has to drive for miles and miles to get here from Scotland."

Their mum came into the room, rubbing her eyes. "Get back to bed, you two," she said crossly. "It's not even six o'clock yet!"

"But Lottie's coming!" Jim said.

"She won't be here until late this

afternoon," Mrs Dodd told him. "And everything is ready. Now come on, back to bed." She led Jim back to his bedroom.

Emma sighed, drew the curtains and climbed back into bed, knowing she wouldn't be able to sleep.

After what seemed like an age,

she gave up and crept downstairs to watch television. Jim was already in the living room, watching cartoons.

But all Emma could think about was Lottie. "Wait till everyone sees her," she sighed happily. Lottie was even better than Duke, Tracey's pony.

Tracey lived next door to Emma and they also went to the same riding school. She was always talking about the brilliant things that Duke could do.

Emma had been having lessons on the school's ponies. But next lesson, she would be riding a pony of her own. She couldn't wait!

Too restless to sit still, Emma

jumped up and ran upstairs to wash and get dressed.

A few minutes later she was outside, checking the shed once more. She patted down the straw that was ready for Lottie to sleep on, and then she checked that they'd bought the right feed for her. Gran had told them what to buy, and she was bringing Lottie's tack, grooming kit and buckets.

At the back door, Emma caught sight of her riding hat and boots. She'd polished the boots the day before until she could almost see her face in them. But there was no harm in polishing them just one more time.

After she'd done that, she went out for a walk around the field.

In the next field, Tracey was getting Duke ready for a ride. "Do you want to come and watch me riding Duke?" she called out.

"I can't," Emma shouted back. "Lottie's coming today!"

"Great!" Tracey called back. "But I bet she's nowhere near as good as Duke," she teased.

"Oh no?" Emma smiled. "Just you wait and see!"

She went back indoors, ate some breakfast then phoned her best friend, Paula. "Come over for tea," she said. "Lottie should be here then."

After that, she phoned another friend, Tania, and invited her over too.

Late that afternoon, Emma stood at the garden gate with Tania and Paula. She looked at her watch. Five o'clock.

She peered down the lane, but there wasn't a trailer in sight. Cars zoomed past in the busy main road in the distance, but nobody turned into their lane.

"I wonder where they are," said Tania.

"Me too," said Emma.

"Do you think they might be lost?" Paula asked.

Emma ran into the house to talk to her mum, who was working at her computer. "Where are they?" she asked. "You said they'd be here before teatime."

"They could be caught in traffic," her mum replied. "Just be patient. It's a very long journey, remember?"

Emma nodded and sighed. "But *roughly* how much longer do you think they'll be?" she asked.

Not too far away, in a slow-moving trailer, Lottie wondered

the same thing. "I'm so hot and bored and tired of being in the dark!" she whinnied. "I wonder how much longer this is going to take?" She stamped her hooves and shuffled about.

The car and trailer slowed down and stopped.

"Have we arrived yet?" Lottie neighed.

But they hadn't. Granny Dodd had just stopped again to check that Lottie was all right. She'd done this quite a lot during the long journey.

"We'll soon be there," she said, patting Lottie gently. "Now be patient."

Emma looked down the lane for

the hundredth time. At last, she saw a car and a trailer turn off the main road and drive slowly down the lane towards her. "They're coming! They're coming. I can see them!" she shouted.

Mr and Mrs Dodd and Jim hurried out to join Emma and her two friends at the garden gate.

In the trailer, Lottie asked herself for the thousandth time, "I wonder if we're nearly there?"

Then the car stopped again.

"Perhaps *this* time," Lottie whickered excitedly. She could hear lots of voices.

Suddenly the ramp was lowered and the dark trailer flooded with sunlight. Granny Dodd climbed in and began to untie Lottie.

"Hooray!" Lottie whinnied. "We're here!"

Slowly, Granny Dodd turned the little pony and led her down the ramp.

Lottie pranced, wanting to see Emma at once. But when she looked at the people lined up to meet her, her heart sank with disappointment. Three big girls stood by the garden gate and she didn't recognise any of them.

"Where's Emma?" she snorted rudely. "Why isn't she here?"

As Emma saw the pony step out of the trailer, her mouth fell open in surprise. Her heart sank with disappointment too. *Is that really Lottie?* she wondered. She looks so *small.*

For a moment there was silence. Lottie stared at three girls, and the three girls stared back.

Granny Dodd's voice rang out. She sounded surprised as well. "Why, Emma, how you've grown!" she said. "You've really shot up since my visit last year."

"Yes, she has," Emma's dad said. "Oh dear, Lottie looks almost too small for Emma now."

One of the girls walked towards Lottie. She was tall and slim and Lottie didn't think she'd ever seen her before, though her sparkling green eyes did look familiar.

The girl flung her arms around Lottie and whispered to her. "Welcome to your new home,

Lottie. I knew we'd be together one day!"

Lottie knew the girl's voice. She whickered in surprise. It really *was* Emma! "Thank you," Lottie snorted, pushing her soft nose against Emma's hand. "But you look so different!"

Just then, they heard some hooves. Tracey was riding up the lane towards them on Duke. "Is *that* Lottie?" she laughed. "You can't ride *her*, Emma. She's tiny!"

Emma went red in the face as she looked at Lottie. "Yes I can!" she called back. "Lottie is just the right size!"

But Emma wasn't so sure about that – and neither was Lottie . . .

Chapter Three

Granny Dodd stayed for the weekend, helping Lottie settle into her new home and showing Emma how to look after her.

Emma was keen to see if she was still able to ride Lottie. It would be awful if she really had grown too much! But she had to wait until

Lottie had rested from the long journey.

The following day, Granny Dodd and Emma's mum brought out Lottie's saddle and bridle and helped Emma to tack up the pony.

Full of excitement, Emma heaved herself up into the saddle.

"Oh dear," Lottie snorted. "You're a bit heavier than you used to be, Emma!"

Emma looked down at her feet and frowned. "I'm going to have to let the stirrups down a lot," she said.

She fiddled with the stirrup leathers until they were the right length, then wriggled about until she felt comfortable.

Emma's mum looked at Granny

Dodd anxiously. "What do you think?" she asked. "Has Emma grown too big for Lottie?"

Granny Dodd scratched her chin. "Hmm," she said thoughtfully. "Walk Lottie around a little, lass," she told Emma.

Emma touched Lottie's sides gently with her heels to let her know it was time to walk on.

Lottie began to move. Carrying Emma on her back was harder work now, but Lottie felt she could manage.

Emma looked over at her gran anxiously. What would she decide?

"Well," said Granny Dodd. "I think that Lottie should be able to carry Emma for a few months at least – but when Emma grows a little more, we'll have to think again."

When Emma heard this she felt both happy and sad. Yes, she could ride Lottie after all. But not for much longer!

Soon it was time for Emma's gran to go. Emma led Lottie round to the front of the house to see her off.

Granny Dodd gave all the family a kiss, then finally turned to hug Lottie. "Now, you be good, lass," she said. "I'll miss you."

"I'll miss you too," Lottie whinnied softly, nuzzling Granny Dodd's cheek. "But don't worry about me. I'm sure I'll be really happy with Emma."

Granny Dodd turned to Emma and hugged her too. "Don't forget to give Lottie lots of praise," she advised. "Ponies like to be told they've done well."

"We certainly do," Lottie whinnied.

Emma hugged her gran back. "I'll phone you and write to you

often," she promised, "to tell you how Lottie's getting on."

"And I'll write to you about Dilly," said Jim, not wanting to be left out. Dilly was the new family kitten, which Jim was clutching to his chest.

"Thank you, dear. I'd like that," said his gran, smiling.

As soon as they had waved her gran off, Emma turned to her mum. "It's almost time to go for my next lesson at the riding school," she said. "The first on my own pony! I can't wait to show Lottie to everyone!"

"Great!" Lottie snorted. "Let's get started. I want to meet the other ponies."

Emma's mum walked with them down the lane to the riding school. Lottie swished her tail and sniffed the air. It was early summer. The trees were thick with leaves, the flowers were in bloom and birds were calling from every branch.

Lottie would have liked to stop

and look at her new surroundings, but Emma wanted to get to the stables in time for the lesson.

Lottie didn't mind. She was just happy to be back with Emma.

At the stables, the ponies and their riders were standing in a circle waiting for the lesson to begin. They all turned to look at Emma arriving on her new little pony.

Suddenly Emma noticed Tracey grinning at her. She began to feel a bit nervous and gently pulled on Lottie's reins to ask her to stop.

Betty Dickson, the instructor, walked across to greet them. "Welcome!" she said. "This must be Lottie. I've heard all about you," she went on, stroking the pony's face. "But Emma didn't say you were such a tiddler!"

Emma's heart sank. Even Mrs Dickson was saying how small Lottie was.

"Don't worry, Emma," the instructor added kindly. "You should be able to ride Lottie for a little while before you grow too big. Come and join the class."

Emma waved goodbye to her mum and rode Lottie over to the circle of ponies and riders.

Lottie whinnied to the other ponies. "Hello, I'm Lottie. I've just come down from Scotland."

"Pleased to meet you," the ponies whinnied back.

One rather large bay pony snorted. "My name is Duke. I

must say, you don't look like you've had much riding practice lately!"

Offended, Lottie snorted back. "So what?" she replied. "I used to belong to a lovely, kind old lady who couldn't ride me any more – but she taught me well, and I still know how to trot and

canter and jump!"

"Go on, then. Show us," Duke urged her.

Without thinking, Lottie lifted her head and darted forwards to show off some of her skills.

Not expecting Lottie to move so quickly, Emma lost both her stirrups and had to grab hold of Lottie's mane to stay on her back.

Lottie felt Emma losing her balance and stopped with a jolt.

"Ha, ha, ha!" one of the riders laughed. It was Tracey. "Emma almost fell off! At least she doesn't have far to fall, riding that titchy thing!"

Emma gave Tracey an annoyed look, pushed her feet back into the stirrups, then bent down to whisper in Lottie's ear. "What's wrong, girl?" she asked.

Embarrassed and ashamed, Lottie pushed her cheek against Emma's. "I'm sorry, Emma. Duke was very rude and I got angry," she blew. "I was trying to show off a bit," she admitted. "But I won't do that again. I promise."

"Right, then," called Mrs Dickson. "Let's get on!"

Chapter Four

With each lesson at the riding school, Emma and Lottie grew a bit more confident together.

But it was clear that soon Emma really would be too big for Lottie.

When the class did exercises – keeping their feet in the stirrups and lying back on their ponies –

Emma's head hung over the top of Lottie's tail!

Lottie didn't mind, and Emma got used to it. But Tracey always called out, "You'll soon be doing backward somersaults!"

Tracey's pony, Duke, would neigh to Lottie, "Don't you feel silly with a big rider like that?"

"No, I don't," Lottie neighed back. "Emma and I make a great team!"

Emma's best friends, Tania and Paula, often came round to help her muck out Lottie's stable and clean her tack. Together they raked over her field, clearing it and weeding it so that Lottie wouldn't eat any harmful plants.

Lottie loved her new life with Emma. And she was right: together they made a great team. Soon Lottie needed only the lightest tap of the heels or pull on the reins from Emma to know exactly what Emma wanted her to do.

So when Mrs Dickson

announced that it would soon be time for the local gymkhana, Emma was one of the first to sign up.

Tracey saw Emma writing down Lottie's name. "You must be daft to enter on that titchy pony of yours," she laughed. "Everyone will think it's a joke!"

Emma went red. "No they won't," she said, hotly. "We'll be as good as everyone else – and perhaps better than you!"

Tracey's laughter echoed in Emma's ears as Tracey wrote her name with Duke's under Emma's and Lottie's.

Later, while she was brushing Lottie, Emma worried about what

Tracey had said. Then something else began to bother her too: Jim had started to hang around Lottie a lot.

Dilly the kitten had grown bored with being held all the time. Now she went out after breakfast and often didn't come back until teatime. So Jim was looking for something new to interest him.

Emma didn't like this at all. She wanted to keep Lottie to herself!

"Why don't you go and look for Dilly?" Emma suggested to her little brother. "Lottie's *my* pony."

"Don't want to," Jim said, giving Lottie a stroke.

Lottie didn't mind. She quite liked Jim.

In the distance, in the field next

door, Emma saw Tracey and Duke jumping over poles.

Tracey shouted out, "Why don't you bring Lottie over? Let's see who can jump the highest."

Emma frowned. Duke was so big, there was no way that Lottie could ever jump as high as him.

"No thanks, we're too busy to jump," Emma replied.

"You're just scared you'll lose!" Tracey called back. "Anyway, even if Lottie *could* jump, she wouldn't be able to with you riding her. You're too heavy. Ponies like Lottie are meant for little kids."

Jim had been listening. "I'm little," he said. "I'll ride Lottie."

"Oh no you won't," Emma snapped back. "You can't ride!" She hugged Lottie's neck. "We don't need to jump," she whispered to Lottie. "We're good at other things. Wait until Tracey sees us at the gymkhana."

Chapter Five

The sun was shining as Emma and Lottie arrived at the gymkhana field. Her friends Tania and Paula had come to watch, as well as her mum, dad and Jim. Ponies and riders had come from all the surrounding villages, and a crowd had gathered to watch the races, jumping competition and displays.

Several heads turned to look at Emma on Lottie, and some people pointed and giggled.

"Take no notice," Emma whispered to Lottie.

"Don't worry. I won't," Lottie whinnied back and tossed her mane. "I'm used to people staring at us. But they'll soon see what a good team we are!"

Emma waited nervously for the first race in her age group to be called. Then she lined up and tried her best to ignore Tracey, who had been placed in the lane next to her.

The first race was Walk, Trot and Canter. The whistle went, and

Emma urged Lottie forward to
walk as quickly as she could
down the track.

Within seconds Tracey and Duke
and some of the other ponies had
pulled ahead. Lottie got to the end
of the track and Emma turned her
round, asking her to trot back
again.

When they'd finished the

trotting section, Lottie cantered back as fast as she could, but her short stride made it impossible for her to keep up with the bigger ponies.

"Rotten luck," Tania and Paula called from the sidelines.

Tracey had won the race and showed off her rosette to everyone. She won the next race, too. As she passed Emma and Lottie she turned and grinned. "Why don't you give up?" she said. "Lottie's too little to compete."

"We'll never give up," Emma said. Then she whispered to Lottie, "Now we really have to go for it."

The bending race was next.

Ponies had to weave in and out of a row of posts.

Being so small, Lottie found it easier than the other ponies to hurry through the spaces between the poles. She wove in and out of the posts with such speed that she seemed to reach the end in no time at all.

Emma was almost dizzy with excitement when she was handed the rosette for first place.

"Well done!" Tania and Paula shouted. "We knew you could do it."

Tracey looked annoyed. "I wasn't ready at the start," she spluttered. "I didn't hear the whistle."

Next came the egg and spoon

race. Once again, Lottie sprang into action.

Emma could hear Duke thundering along beside her in the next lane. But Tracey made Duke go so fast that she dropped her egg and had to leave the race.

Somehow Lottie kept her nerve and, cantering smoothly and steadily, she came in first again.

"Hurrah!" Paula and Tania shouted. "You and Lottie are even with Tracey and Duke now. You've won the same number of races!"

It was time for the final event – the sack race. The ponies had to trot with their riders to one end of the track, then the riders jumped back in a sack, leading their ponies.

Emma knew that Lottie's short legs wouldn't let her trot as fast as other, larger ponies like Duke.

But when the whistle went, Lottie, who was having a great time and not nervous at all, got off to a good start. As they reached the far end, Lottie was a little behind Duke. As quickly as she could, Emma leaped out of the saddle and wriggled into the sack. Then she jumped forward with huge, hopping leaps. Emma's long legs were coming in useful!

From the sidelines Emma could hear her friends and family calling, "Go for it, Emma!"

With one last almighty leap, she jumped over the finishing line into first place.

Tracey crashed into second place behind her.

Emma could hardly believe it. Together, she and Lottie had won the final race! In fact, they had won more events than anyone else. Emma and Lottie were champions of the gymkhana!

"Yaaay! You've won, Emma!" yelled Jim, rushing up to her and Lottie. Mr and Mrs Dodd followed, smiling proudly.

"She's my sister!" Jim shouted, to anyone who would listen.

"Well done, Emma. That was fantastic," said Betty Dickson as she walked up to them. "And well done, Lottie!" she added, stroking Lottie's mane. "What a great team!"

"Thanks!" Lottie snorted. She was a bit hot and tired.

Just then, someone tapped Emma's shoulder. Emma turned round and saw that it was Tracey. Her heart sank. Was Tracey going to spoil her and Lottie's big moment?

But to Emma's surprise, Tracey said quietly, "I feel a bit silly now for being so rude about you and Lottie. You were both great today."

Emma was too surprised to say anything back. Tracey turned and began to walk quickly away.

"Tracey!" Emma shouted. "So were you and Duke!"

Tracey turned back and smiled, then went over to where her

family and Duke were waiting.

"That was very kind of you, Emma," said Mrs Dickson, quietly. "It took a lot of courage for Tracey to say that."

The next day, when Emma came in from school, her mum smiled at her very oddly. Then she said, "I spoke with Granny Dodd earlier and she'd like you to give her a ring."

Emma had tried to phone her gran when she'd arrived home from the gymkhana, but there had been no answer.

This time, Granny Dodd answered straight away.

"Did Mum tell you, Gran? Lottie did brilliantly!" Emma said

proudly. "Though it was kind of tough for her, me being so big," she added.

"You *both* did brilliantly," her gran agreed. "And I'm glad you and Lottie had the chance to win together." Then she added gently, "Because you know that you will be too big to ride Lottie in next year's gymkhana, don't you, lass?"

Emma nodded sadly. "Yes, Gran, but what about Lottie?" she asked worriedly. "You wanted her to come and live with us so that there would be someone to ride her and have fun with her."

"Well," her gran said, "I expect Jim will be wanting to learn to ride now. Maybe you could help him. And . . ." Granny Dodd stopped for a moment.

Emma wondered what she was going to say.

"And there's enough room in the field next to your new house for another pony, isn't there?" Granny Dodd asked.

Emma could tell her gran was smiling. "Yes . . ." she agreed slowly. "Why?"

"Well," explained Granny Dodd, "when you called yesterday, I was out talking with my neighbour, Mr Stewart, who owns Noah. You know, the pony who used to share Lottie's field."

"Oh, yes, I remember," said Emma. "Noah's lovely, too. He isn't a Shetland, though – he's much bigger than Lottie."

"Exactly," said her gran. "And when Mr Stewart told me that he had to find a new home for Noah, I had a marvellous idea . . ."

Emma stood by the back door, watching Jim feed handfuls of grass to Lottie. She was thinking hard. She had wanted Lottie for so long, and in her dreams she'd had Lottie all to herself. She hadn't expected to have to share her!

But it was true that soon she wouldn't be able to ride Lottie any more. And her mum and dad had agreed that Granny Dodd's idea was a good one: if Emma wanted Noah, he could come and share a field with Lottie again. He could

belong to Emma!

Emma took a deep breath and went out to the field, picking up Lottie's tack on the way.

"Hey, Jim. How would you like to learn to ride?" she asked.

"On Lottie?" Jim's eyes opened wide. "Will you teach me? Really?" He flung his arms around her.

Emma nodded. "As long as Lottie doesn't mind," she added quickly.

"Of course I don't mind," Lottie whickered. She nuzzled Emma's arm.

Emma patted Lottie gently and a big smile spread across her face. Perhaps things would work out OK. Lottie would love having Noah around too!

She began to show Jim how to tack up, and when they were finished, she lifted him onto Lottie's broad back.

Emma smiled. Jim looked just right for Lottie. Having a little brother had its uses after all!